While Daddy is Away
Days of Deployment

TWO GIRLS AND A READING CORNER

Two Girls and a Reading Corner

www.twogirlsandareadingcorner.com

WHILE DADDY IS AWAY,
DAYS OF DEPLOYMENT
TWO GIRLS AND A READING CORNER
Copyright © 2021 TRISTA LAWRENCE
ISBN: 978-1-952879-38-8
Cover Art and Illustrations by DENNY POLIQUIT
Edited by MELANIE LOPATA

For permission requests, please email
twogirlsandareadingcorner@gmail.com
Place "Request for Permissions" in the subject line or contact:
Two Girls and a Reading Corner
PO Box 2404, Madison, AL 35758

First and foremost, all the glory and thanks to God for choosing me as His vessel. This book is His; I just put the pen to paper. On behalf of the team of Two Girls and a Reading Corner and myself, we would like to thank those who have served and are currently serving—as well as the families who stand behind them—for our freedom.

-WE SUPPORT OUR TROOPS-

A special recognition to my father, MSgt. Thomas D. Keller, who retired after serving 21 years in the Air Force.

Thank you for being the selfless, God-fearing man you are and putting your family and country first.

I am proud to be your daughter.

My parents told us Daddy has to go

away for work for a long time.

He travels to other places to help people, and that makes us proud of him. Daddy is so brave.

While Daddy is away, we help

Mommy with chores around the house.

We help her with grocery shopping.

We even help Mommy take care of our little brother.

Sometimes Mommy lets us pick out
treats to send to Daddy.

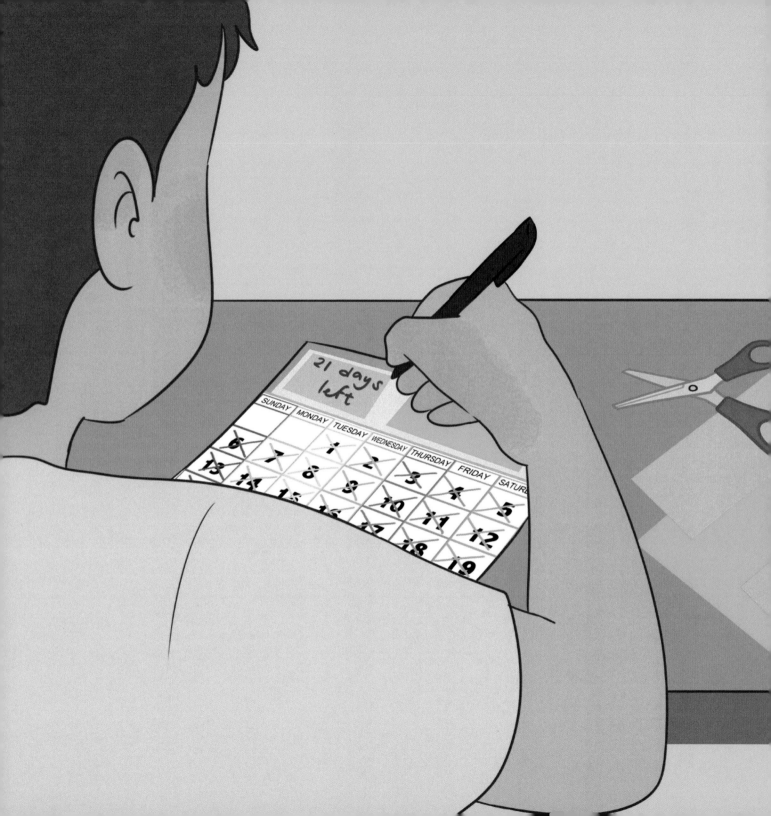

While Daddy is away, we make a countdown calendar, so we can cross off the days until he comes home.

We talk to Daddy as often as we are able.

We get excited for his phone calls.

He says he thinks about us every day.

When we're really missing our daddy, we draw pictures for him and send them in the mail. Our pictures make him feel special.

While Daddy is away, we stay busy doing the things that we love. It makes him happy to know that we are having fun.

It's okay to feel sad that Daddy is gone.

It helps to talk about it with our mommy.

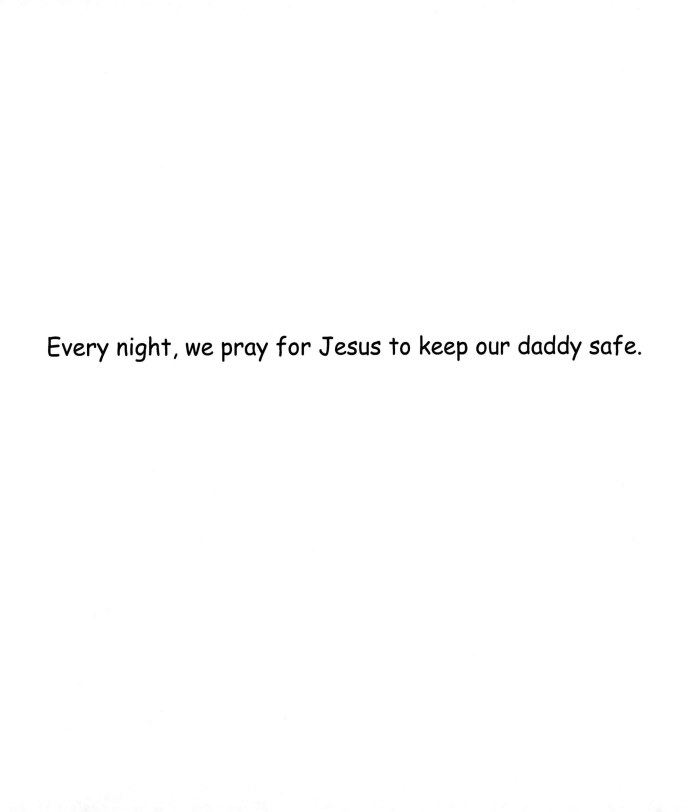

Every night, we pray for Jesus to keep our daddy safe.

It's almost time for Daddy to come home.

We're going to make him a "Welcome Home" sign.

We can use patriotic colors; he'll love that.

Welcome home, Daddy. We want
to grow up and be as brave as you.

The End

Acknowledgments

I want to thank the hard-working team of Two Girls and a Reading Corner. To Mandy, who has been by my writing side for three books now and has been nothing but the best cheerleader and friend. To Denny and her gift of art; without your gift, this book couldn't come to life. To my rocks: Brooklyn, Brynli, Turner, Collins, Michael, and most importantly, all the Glory to God, for this book isn't really from me, but from Him. It's His world, I just live in it.

About the Author

Trista Lawrence is from Fort Walton Beach, Florida and currently resides in a small town near Huntsville, Alabama with her beautiful family. She prides herself on being a mother and entrepreneur. When she's not writing, she's enjoying her family, friends, job, and photography.
"Life is too short to sweat the small stuff.
I just love to laugh and hope to inspire others.
Most importantly, bring them to know Jesus like I do.
It's a game changer for sure."

About the Illustrator

Denny Poliquit is a children's book illustrator and a typography designer. She has an Associate's degree in computer technology, majoring in animation. She spends most of her time working and developing herskills and passion in designing. She always wants to share her knowledge and skills for the success for her authors and clients.

Also, by Trista Lawrence:

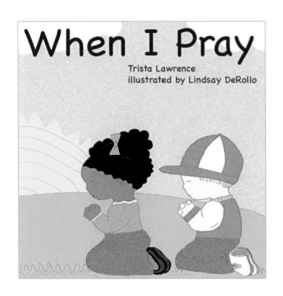

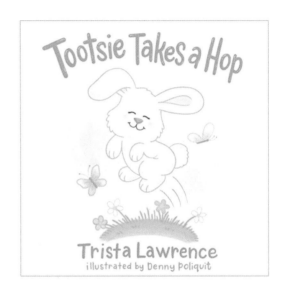

For details about our books and upcoming releases;
visit our website
www.twogirlsandareadingcorner.com

Two Girls and a Reading Corner

P.O. Box 2404

Madison, AL 35758

Made in the USA
Middletown, DE
27 January 2023